P9-AZV-703

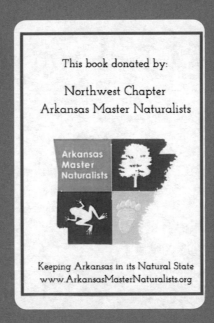

This book donated by:

Northwest Chapter
Arkansas Master Naturalists

Keeping Arkansas in its Natural State
www.ArkansasMasterNaturalists.org

Springdale Public Library
405 S. Pleasant
Springdale, AR 72764

INSECTS ARE MY LIFE

story by Megan McDonald

pictures by Paul Brett Johnson

Orchard Books • New York
An Imprint of Scholastic Inc.

Springdale Public Library
405 S. Pleasant
Springdale, AR 72764

No part of this publication may be reproduced in whole or in part, or stored in a retrieval system, or transmitted in any form or by any means, electronic, mechanical, photocopying, recording, or otherwise, without written permission of the publisher. For information regarding permission, write to Orchard Books, Scholastic Inc., Attention: Permissions Department, 557 Broadway, New York, NY 10012.

Text copyright © 1995 by Megan McDonald. Illustrations copyright © 1995 by Paul Brett Johnson. All rights reserved. Published by Orchard Books, an imprint of Scholastic Inc. ORCHARD BOOKS and design are registered trademarks of Watts Publishing Group, Ltd., used under license. SCHOLASTIC and associated logos are trademarks and/or registered trademarks of Scholastic Inc.

Library of Congress Cataloging-in-Publication Data
McDonald, Megan. Insects are my life / story by Megan McDonald; pictures by Paul Brett Johnson.
   p. cm.
Summary: No one at home or school understands Amanda Frankenstein's devotion to insects until she meets Maggie.
ISBN 0-531-06874-9 (tr.) ISBN 0-531-08724-7 (lib. bdg.)
[1. Insects—Fiction. 2. Schools—Fiction. 3. Family life—Fiction.] I. Johnson, Paul Brett, ill.
II. Title PZ7.M478419In 1995
[E]—dc20 94-21960
10 9 8 7 6 5   04 05 06 07 08

Printed in Singapore 46
First Orchard Paperbacks edition 1997.
The text of this book is set in 15 point Usherwood Medium.
The illustrations are watercolor, colored pencil, and pastel reproduced in full color.
Book design by Mina Greenstein.

To Dick, for seeing

—M.M.

For Cheryl and Steve

—P.B.J.

The night that Andrew caught the fireflies in a jar, Amanda set them all free.

That was the first real clue that Amanda Frankenstein was crazy about insects. Bugs. Dozens of bugs. Cousins of bugs. Big bugs. Small bugs. Any bugs. All bugs. Creepy bugs. Crawly bugs. Slimy bugs. Climby bugs. Bugs with wings. Bugs that sing.

"How would *you* like to live in a peanut butter jar?" she asked her brother. "Bugs are people, too, you know!"

That night, she drew a giant dragonfly on the dinosaur poster in his room. And she slipped her ugliest rubber cockroach under his pillow before bed.

Amanda examined bugs. With her detective kit. Under rocks, hidden on leaves, in sidewalk cracks. She counted eleven different kinds in a single afternoon, including a seven-spotted ladybug.

Springdale Public Library
405 S. Pleasant
Springdale, AR 72764

Amanda collected bugs. Dead ones, of course. The skin of a grasshopper, the shell of a cicada, a perfect pair of dragonfly wings found after a thunderstorm. She collected bug cases. Once she hatched hundreds of tiny praying mantises right in her sock drawer. She collected mosquito bites. She counted twenty-two bites on one leg, and she was proud.

Amanda Frankenstein was a bug's best friend. She always stepped *around* spiderwebs. She hid the flyswatter. She rescued five ants from getting stepped on in the kitchen. She clicked her tongue at bats to confuse them and keep them from eating so many insects.

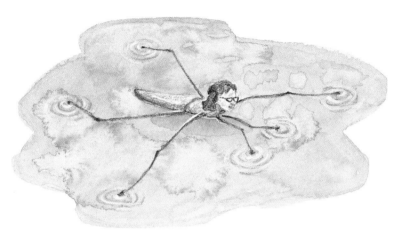

Amanda dreamed of
hanging upside down on
the ceiling like a fly. She
imagined walking on
water as nimbly as a water strider. Once she tried crawling forty
miles on all fours, like an ant, and got as far as the backyard fence.
"That's how far an ant could walk if it was a person!" she explained
when her mother called her inside.

"Find something else to do until dinner, Amanda."

So Amanda watched her favorite movie, *The Fly,* two times in a row.

"My sister, the insect," said her brother. Amanda ignored him. Tonight, he would find her trick ice cube in his milk. The one with the dead fly in the center.

The End

After dark, Amanda opened her window wide and turned on the light so all the night bugs would fly in. She spied a yellow hawk moth, a garden tiger moth, and a lacewing fly. That is, until her mother found out. Thanks to Andrew.

"No bugs in the house, Amanda. When you're old enough to have your own house, you can have all the bugs you want there."

"When I'm all grown up, I'm going to be an entomologist," she told her mother, "and hatch rare butterflies in my living room."

"You can't be *that,*" said her brother.

"Then you can't be a dead bone digger either!"

"Paleontologist. They study dinosaurs. Dinosaurs are neat. Bugs are slimy."

"*Insects* are not slimy. Insects are
fascinating. Insects are my life!"

On the first day of school, Amanda's mother begged her to wear her blue dress with the pink flowers. But Amanda insisted on wearing her ladybug T-shirt that said, AMANDA FRANKENSTEIN: FRIEND OF BUGS. She carried her new magnifying glass in a special pocket of her backpack. And she wore her purple dragonfly pin for good luck.

Ms. Scorpio, her teacher, had a dress the color of a luna moth
and hair like a beehive. She led the class in a song,

"The ants go marching one by one, Hurrah! Hooray!
The last one stops to suck her thumb . . ."

and Amanda sang the loudest.

Springdale Public Librar
405 S. Pleasant
Springdale, AR 72764

When it was time to choose an instrument to play, Amanda chose the triangle.

"You'll have to share with Victor," Ms. Scorpio told her. Victor had squinty little eyes like a slug and two spikes of hair that acted like antennae.

"Can you use those to smell?" Amanda asked.

"Bug off, Bug-eyes!" he hissed, pointing to her glasses.

The other kids laughed. "Four eyes! Four eyes!" they chanted. "Amanda has four eyes!"

"They're compound eyes," Amanda told them. "Like a wasp's." After that, Amanda played the tambourine. By herself.

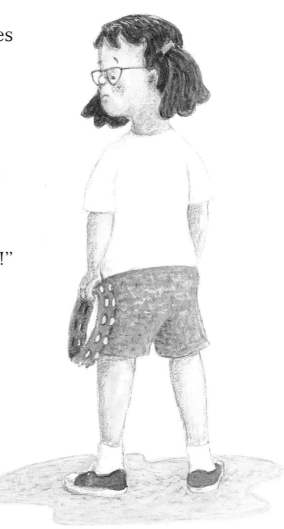

The teacher took them on a bear hunt, over mountains, through forests. "I see . . . a cave. Can't go over it. Can't go around it. Have to go through it!" Amanda pretended with the others to look for a bear, but secretly she searched for an African killer beetle.

During circle time, Ms. Scorpio read *The Very Quiet Cricket*,
and Amanda made the cricket sound, *"Cree! Cree! Cree!"*

When it came her turn to recite a poem, Amanda made one
up:

"Bugs are great
Bugs are good
Bugs live in your neighborhood."

That afternoon, Victor put a hairy spider on her seat. Amanda held it in her hand and pulled out her magnifying glass to study it. "A wolf spider!" she announced excitedly. "Did you know spiders are arthropods?"

"Amanda Frankenstein, you are a monster," Victor said.

"And you, Victor, are less than a flea. You are a stinkbug on the leaf of life."

"All right, that's enough. Time out for both of you."

Amanda had to sit in a chair and face the wall for ten minutes because of Victor. Tomorrow, Victor would find a Chinese water bug in his lunch box.

"I'm never
going back to
school," Amanda
announced when
she got home. She
wrapped herself in a
blanket and hid inside
her cocoon. She tasted
leaves and bark. She
painted butterfly wings
with eyespots like owls
on them to scare away
animals. And creeps like
Victor. She tied the wings
to her arms and flew
down three steps.
"First to fly!" she
called.

"Amanda Frankenstein, get your feet off the table!" her mother scolded at dinner that night.

"But butterflies have taste buds on their feet," Amanda said.

"Well, please keep your taste buds on the floor," said her mother.

The next day was worse. When Amanda danced in circles like a bee, no other bees followed. When she pulled out her Mexican jumping beans for show-and-tell, no one believed there were caterpillars inside. And when Amanda pretended to have ears on her knees, like a cricket, the teacher told her to sit up straight and listen.

"Amanda Frankenstein thinks she's a bug!" yelled Victor. "A cricket! *Cree! Cree!*"

"Victor, you are a worm." Amanda told him.

"I thought you liked bugs."

"Worms are not insects, Victor."

"How do you know?"

"Because. Insects are my life!"

"Not again, you two. Amanda, come sit over here by Maggie today."

"I like your glasses," whispered Amanda.

"They're for seeing underwater," Maggie said.

"Like whirligig beetles?" asked Amanda.

"Like crocodiles!" Maggie grinned widely, showing two pointy teeth. "Reptiles are my life!"